C D E F
K L M N
S T U V
Z

I dedicate this book to that tireless group of *alphabet purveyors*: our teachers.—A.K.R.

To Chamo and Yassine.—D.D.

G. P. PUTNAM'S SONS A division of Penguin Young Readers Group.
Published by The Penguin Group. Penguin Group (USA) Inc., 375 Hudson Street, New York, NY 10014, U.S.A.
Penguin Group (Canada), 90 Eglinton Avenue East, Suite 700, Toronto, Ontario M4P 2Y3, Canada
(a division of Pearson Penguin Canada Inc.).
Penguin Books Ltd, 80 Strand, London WC2R 0RL, England.
Penguin Ireland, 25 St. Stephen's Green, Dublin 2, Ireland (a division of Penguin Books Ltd.).
Penguin Group (Australia), 250 Camberwell Road, Camberwell, Victoria 3124, Australia
(a division of Pearson Australia Group Pty Ltd).
Penguin Books India Pvt Ltd, 11 Community Centre, Panchsheel Park, New Delhi - 110 017, India.
Penguin Group (NZ), 67 Apollo Drive, Rosedale, North Shore 0632, New Zealand (a division of Pearson New Zealand Ltd).
Penguin Books (South Africa) (Pty) Ltd, 24 Sturdee Avenue, Rosebank, Johannesburg 2196, South Africa.
Penguin Books Ltd, Registered Offices: 80 Strand, London WC2R 0RL, England.

Published simultaneously in Canada. Manufactured in China by South China Printing Co. Ltd.

Design by Ryan Thomann. Text set in Bleeker.
The art was done in acrylic.

Library of Congress Cataloging-in-Publication Data is available upon request.
ISBN 978-0-399-24601-2
10 9 8 7 6 5 4 3 2 1

G. P. PUTNAM'S SONS · AN IMPRINT OF PENGUIN GROUP (USA) INC.

A long time ago,

there lived a man named Al Pha.

Al lived back when all sorts of things were being invented. Like fire. The wheel. Shadows. Al wanted to invent something too.

One day shortly after the twenty-six letters had been invented, the king announced that they needed to be put into some kind of order. They were thrown together without any rhyme or reason.

"Once the letters are organized, writing will really take off! Books! Poetry! Love letters! Stop signs! Whoever comes up with the most beautiful arrangement for these twenty-six letters will be remembered for all of time," promised the king.

I will do it, Al said to himself excitedly.

He didn't tell anyone that he was going to try. Instead, he made a private bet with himself.

The very next day, Al went to the king's palace to pick up a bag of letters. He took them home and got right to work.

Twenty-six letters.

"That sure is a lot of letters," he said.

The first one was easy. He chose A, for Al.

One down, twenty-five more to go.

Just then, a bee buzzed by.

"Oh no," shrieked Al. "A bee!"

"Hey, that's it.

A. B. Thanks, bee!"

Because Al loved rhyming, he wanted to make sure some letters rhymed. So he grabbed three letters that rhymed with B. C. D. E.

ABCDE

Then Al's twin neighbors passed by. He could never tell them apart. And that's when he noticed: E and F looked almost identical. "Twins do belong together," said Al.

ABCDEF

"Gee, this isn't so hard," said Al. "Gee, I am really doing it. G—that can be the next letter!"

Al's friend Jay strolled by and said, "Hi, Al."

"Hi, Jay. Hi, Jay? Yes, indeed: HI, J!"

Al sure is happy to see me, thought Jay.

"Well, okay, Al,
see you tomorrow."

"What did you say?"

"I just said, 'kay, Al,
see you tomor—"

" 'Kay, Al . . . that's it!
K, L! You're the best!"

"Uh, thanks, I guess,"
Jay said.

ABCDEFGHIJ KL

Feeling hungry, Al picked an apple.

"Mmmm. Delicious."

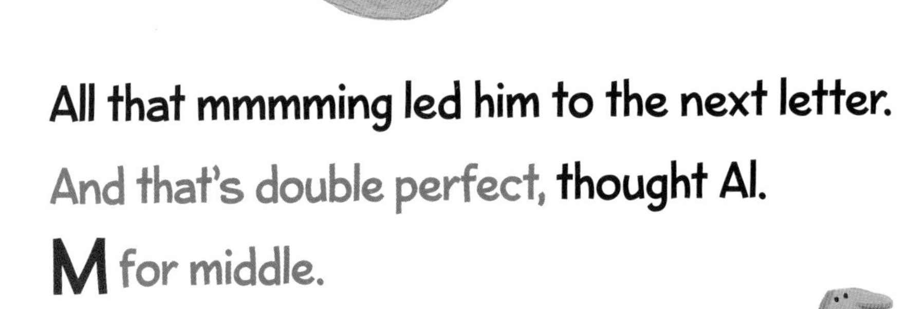

All that mmmming led him to the next letter.

And that's double perfect, thought Al.

M for middle.

He was halfway through!

ABCDEFGHIJKLM

Al had arranged thirteen letters. That meant thirteen more. He was getting tired. He thought about quitting.

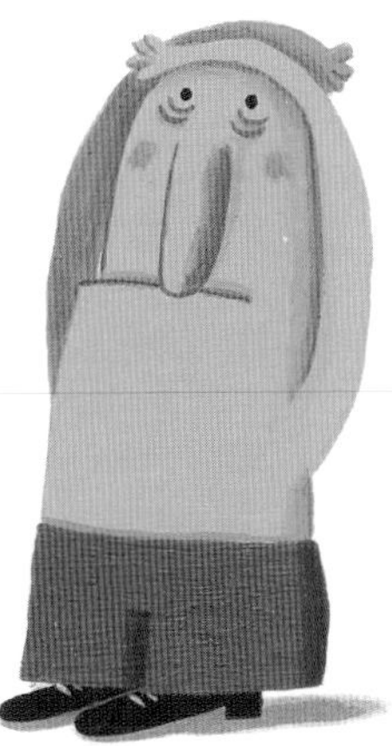

But he remembered the bet he had made with himself. I will keep going. I won't give up. No, no, no.

So he put the N next to the O as a big reminder. No giving up.

ABCDEFGHIJKLMNO

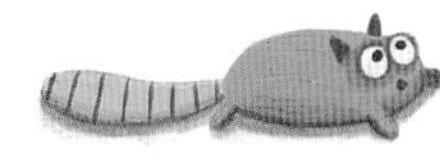

Just then, nature called.

And when Al returned, he knew just what his next letter would be.

P, he said to himself with a smile.

"Now, what next?" he said.

And at that moment a little bird landed on one of the letters, right on cue. Literally.

"Well, Q it is, feathered fellow."

ABCDEFGHIJKLMNOPQ

No sooner had the bird flown away than a snake appeared.

"Arrrrrrrrrr," said Al, trying to scare him off.

"Sssssssssss," sneered the snake.

"Arrrrrrrrrr," said Al.

"Sssssssssss," repeated the snake.

"Hold on, that's it! R, S,"
Al said as the snake slithered away.

ABCDEFGHIJKLMNOPQ RS

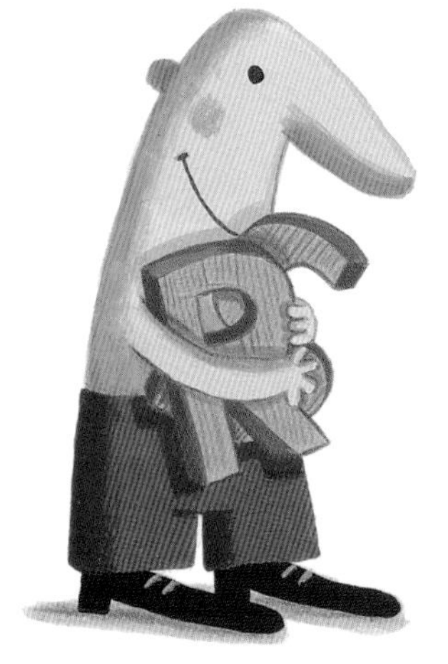

Soon it was Al's favorite time of day.

"Tea time," said Al. And T it was.

ABCDEFGHIJKLMNOPQRST

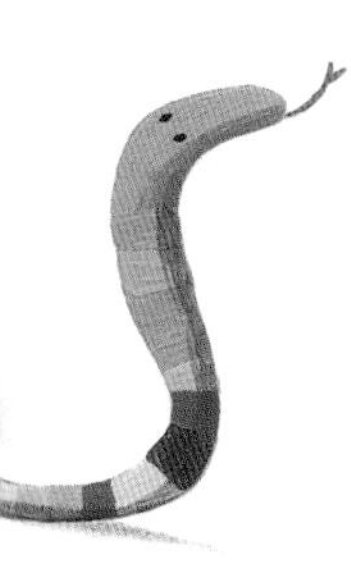

Sipping his tea, Al gave himself a little pep talk.

"You're almost done, Al.

You can DO THIS.

I know you have what it takes.

I know you . . .

I know: U!"

ABCDEFGHIJKLMNOPQRSTU

Only five letters remained.

Al decided to lie down and think.

An inchworm was climbing on the branch above him.

"He looks just like a V and a W

stuck together," Al said.

"That's it! Thank you, my little VW bug!"

ABCDEFGHIJKLMNOPQRSTUVW

The last three now! Al was sooooo close! But oh, how sleepy he was. X next? Z next? Y next? He yawned and rubbed his eyes. Z . . . Z . . . Z . . . ?

Al fell sound asleep. He began snoring. ZZZZZZZZZ . . .

When his own snoring woke him up, he had a brilliant thought: Just as at the end of the day there is sleep, at the end of the letters there shall be Z.

ABCDEFGHIJKLMNOPQRSTUVW. . . Z

Only X and Y remained. He threw them up in the air. "Whichever letter hits the ground first goes after W," he said.

X, being heavier, landed with a thud. So X, then Y it was.

A B C D E F G H I J K L M N O P Q R S T U V W X Y Z

Al did it!

He took his masterpiece to the king.

The king took a good, hard look.

The king said it out loud.

The king tried singing it.

ABCDEFG
HIJKLMNOP
QRSTUV
WXY
and Z

The king wanted to sing it again. He said to Al, “This time, won’t you sing with me?”

Everyone listened as the king and Al sang. It sounded beautiful.

The king proclaimed, "You've done it.
This is the loveliest arrangement I've seen.
I daresay it's even perfect. Tell me, what
is your name, and how did you do it?"

“Your majesty, my name is Al Pha and I made a bet with myself. I said, ‘Al Pha, I bet you can do this. I know you can do this!’ And that, King sir, is what I did.”

“Well,” said the king, “I hereby declare that the twenty-six letters shall be named in honor of Al Pha and his bet!”

And that is how it came to be known as the **Al Pha Bet**.

A B
G H I J
O P Q R
W X Y and